YOUR NAME:
_____

The Elder Scrolls V
SKYRIM

The Elder Scrolls V
SKYRIM

The Elder Scrolls V

SKYRIM

The Elder Scrolls V

SKYRIM

The Elder Scrolls V
SKYRIM

The Elder Scrolls V
SKYRIM

The Elder Scrolls V

SKYRIM

The Elder Scrolls V

SKYRIM

The Elder Scrolls V
SKYRIM

The Elder Scrolls V

SKYRIM

The Elder Scrolls V

SKYRIM

The Elder Scrolls V

SKYRIM

The Elder Scrolls V
SKYRIM

The Elder Scrolls V

SKYRIM

The Elder Scrolls V
SKYRIM

The Elder Scrolls V

SKYRIM

The Elder Scrolls V

SKYRIM

The Elder Scrolls V

SKYRIM

The Elder Scrolls V

SKYRIM

The Elder Scrolls V

SKYRIM

The Elder Scrolls V

SKYRIM

The Elder Scrolls V

SKYRIM

The Elder Scrolls V
SKYRIM

The Elder Scrolls V

SKYRIM

The Elder Scrolls V

SKYRIM

The Elder Scrolls V

SKYRIM

The Elder Scrolls V

SKYRIM

The Elder Scrolls V
SKYRIM

The Elder Scrolls V

SKYRIM

The Elder Scrolls V

SKYRIM

The Elder Scrolls V
SKYRIM

The Elder Scrolls V

SKYRIM

The Elder Scrolls V

SKYRIM

The Elder Scrolls V

SKYRIM

The Elder Scrolls V

SKYRIM

The Elder Scrolls V

SKYRIM

The Elder Scrolls V
SKYRIM

The Elder Scrolls V

SKYRIM

The Elder Scrolls V

SKYRIM

The Elder Scrolls V

SKYRIM

The Elder Scrolls V

SKYRIM

The Elder Scrolls V

SKYRIM

The Elder Scrolls V

SKYRIM

The Elder Scrolls V

SKYRIM

The Elder Scrolls V

SKYRIM

The Elder Scrolls V

SKYRIM

The Elder Scrolls V

SKYRIM

The Elder Scrolls V

SKYRIM

The Elder Scrolls V

SKYRIM

The Elder Scrolls V

SKYRIM

The Elder Scrolls V

SKYRIM

The Elder Scrolls V

SKYRIM

The Elder Scrolls V

SKYRIM

The Elder Scrolls V
SKYRIM

The Elder Scrolls V

SKYRIM

The Elder Scrolls V

SKYRIM

The Elder Scrolls V

SKYRIM

The Elder Scrolls V

SKYRIM

The Elder Scrolls V
SKYRIM

The Elder Scrolls V

SKYRIM

The Elder Scrolls V
SKYRIM

The Elder Scrolls V

SKYRIM

The Elder Scrolls V

SKYRIM

The Elder Scrolls V
SKYRIM

The Elder Scrolls V

SKYRIM

The Elder Scrolls V

SKYRIM

The Elder Scrolls V

SKYRIM

The Elder Scrolls V

SKYRIM

The Elder Scrolls V

SKYRIM

The Elder Scrolls V

SKYRIM

The Elder Scrolls V

SKYRIM

The Elder Scrolls V

SKYRIM

The Elder Scrolls V

SKYRIM

The Elder Scrolls V

SKYRIM

The Elder Scrolls V
SKYRIM

The Elder Scrolls V

SKYRIM

The Elder Scrolls V

SKYRIM

The Elder Scrolls V

SKYRIM

The Elder Scrolls V
SKYRIM

The Elder Scrolls V

SKYRIM

The Elder Scrolls V
SKYRIM

The Elder Scrolls V

SKYRIM

The Elder Scrolls V

SKYRIM

The Elder Scrolls V

SKYRIM

The Elder Scrolls V

SKYRIM

The Elder Scrolls V

SKYRIM

The Elder Scrolls V
SKYRIM

The Elder Scrolls V

SKYRIM

The Elder Scrolls V

SKYRIM

The Elder Scrolls V

SKYRIM

The Elder Scrolls V

SKYRIM

The Elder Scrolls V

SKYRIM

The Elder Scrolls V

SKYRIM

The Elder Scrolls V
SKYRIM

The Elder Scrolls V

SKYRIM

The Elder Scrolls V

SKYRIM

The Elder Scrolls V

SKYRIM

The Elder Scrolls V

SKYRIM

The Elder Scrolls V

SKYRIM

The Elder Scrolls V

SKYRIM

The Elder Scrolls V
SKYRIM

The Elder Scrolls V

SKYRIM

The Elder Scrolls V
SKYRIM

The Elder Scrolls V

SKYRIM

The Elder Scrolls V

SKYRIM

The Elder Scrolls V

SKYRIM

The Elder Scrolls V

SKYRIM

The Elder Scrolls V

SKYRIM

The Elder Scrolls V

SKYRIM

The Elder Scrolls V

SKYRIM

The Elder Scrolls V

SKYRIM

The Elder Scrolls V

SKYRIM

The Elder Scrolls V
SKYRIM

The Elder Scrolls V

SKYRIM

The Elder Scrolls V

SKYRIM

The Elder Scrolls V

SKYRIM

The Elder Scrolls V
SKYRIM

The Elder Scrolls V

SKYRIM

The Elder Scrolls V

SKYRIM

The Elder Scrolls V

SKYRIM

Printed in Great Britain
by Amazon